The Magic is in You

A Magic Wand Story

Written by Carole LaPlante

Illustrated by Mary Ann Byrne-Walker

The Magic is in You

For information about special discounts for bulk purchases, please contact Sunbury Press, Inc. Wholesale Dept. at (717) 254-7274 or orders@sunburypress.com.

To request one of our authors for speaking engagements or book signings, please contact Sunbury Press, Inc. Publicity Dept. at publicity@sunburypress.com.

FIRST SUNBURY PRESS EDITION
Printed in the United States of America
May 2012

ISBN 978-1-62006-055-1

Published by:
Sunbury Press, Inc.
2200 Market Street
Camp Hill, PA   17011

www.sunburypress.com

Camp Hill, Pennsylvania   USA

Dedicated with love to Anna, David, Sidonie. Ryan, Allison, Elijah, Shawnee, Jericho. Cailyn, Christina, Michael, Sophia, Eve, Marley, Sami Jo, Linda Sue, Emily, Angela, Jesse, Tyler, in memory of Jared, and to all the Happy Hollow kids; past, present and future.

"Imagination will often carry us to worlds that never were, but without it we go nowhere."

--- Carl Sagan

Words are the most inexhaustable source of magic.

--- Albus Dumbledore

FOREWORD

THIS IS A TRIBUTE TO THE POWER OF A CHILD'S IMAGINATION. IT WAS THE author's intent to help cultivate this incredible gift that lies within each child on many levels. The ability to turn a plain block into a boat, a doorknob into a water spigot, a bicycle pump into a vacuum cleaner, is the very essence of childhood.

ONCE UPON A TIME, a long long time ago, a very clever fairy godmother invented the magic wand. She wanted to make a very special gift for a special child that she loved very much... someone like YOU as a matter of fact!

Since that time, many other people have tried to make magic wands. They have made them in all sizes and colors, but most are fake and do not possess real magic.

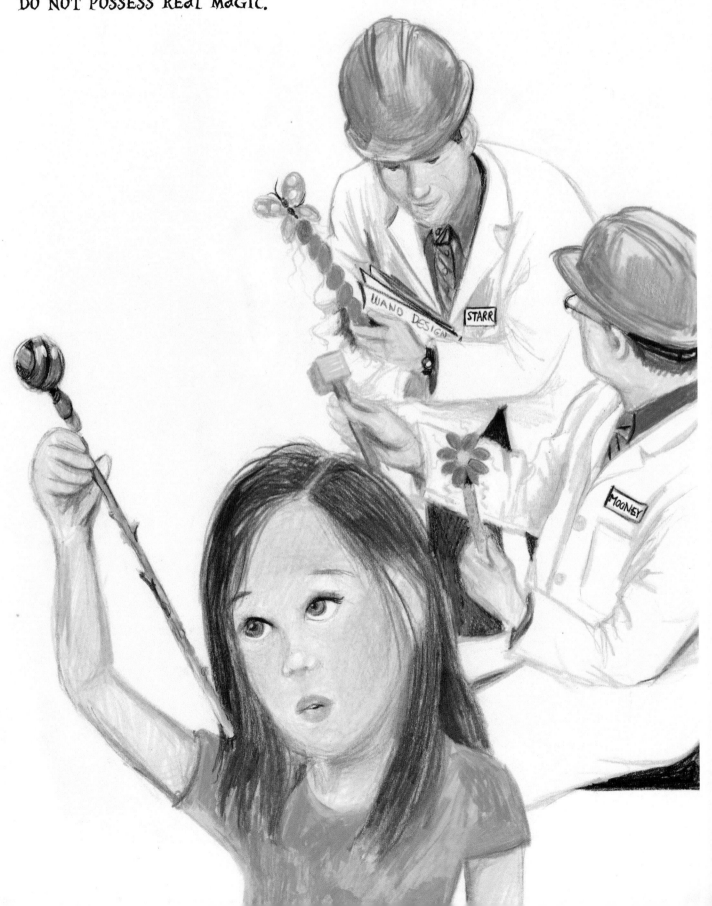

LISTEN CAREFULLY NOW, TO THE INSTRUCTIONS FOR THE CARE AND USE OF THE MOST MAGICAL AND WONDROUSLY REAL MAGIC WAND.

FIRST, YOU ALWAYS NEED TO REMEMBER THAT THE WAND WILL NOT WORK IF YOU DO NOT BELIEVE IN IT. THE MAGIC CAN ONLY COME FROM YOUR IMAGINATION, AND... OF COURSE... THAT LIES WITHIN YOU.

SECONDLY, IT OFTEN HELPS IF YOU DRESS UP TO USE IT. IT IS NOT ABSOLUTELY NECESSARY TO DRESS TOTALLY FANCY, BUT IT HELPS. IT WORKS ESPECIALLY WELL IF PEOPLE DRESSED LIKE, YOU KNOW: QUEENS, KINGS, PRINCESSES, PRINCES, KNIGHTS, GOOD WITCHES, SUPER HEROES AND FAIRIES.

THIRDLY, you can use fairy dust if you want, but you don't really need it. Remember, if you have a good imagination, you can just pretend you have fairy dust at any time and no one will have to sneeze because fairy dust tickles noses! ACHOOOO!!!!

Here are some ideas to help you get started: Think about a wonderful place to be and imagine you are there...

INSIDE OR OUTSIDE, IT DOESN'T MATTER, AS LONG AS EVERYTHING IS INTERESTING OR BEAUTIFUL TO LOOK AT...

... a CASTLE IN THE CLOUDS...

... OR a SEA CAVE...

... OR a FOREST FILLED WITH BEAUTIFUL TREES AND ANIMALS...

... OR a COTTAGE IN THE WOODS...

... OR a
MAGNIFICENT
GARDEN.

Your wand will work
extremely well with music.
The absolute best music to play when
using your wand is ballet stuff or
symphonies. It is hard to concentrate
on the magic if the music is too loud or
has a jerky beat. The music should have a
nice flow to it, like a long smooth letter "s".

Now, let me tell you some of the cool things this wand can do!
If you like to plant things, and have a little garden, you can
wave your wand over the seeds, AND THEY WILL GROW!
If you remember to pull the weeds and water them, they will
grow even bigger and better, but you must be patient, too.

If you are very gentle and careful, and wave the wand over a little brother's toes, HE WILL GROW TOO! Now, of course, this will not happen all at once, but a little brother will grow bigger because of your magic.

Watch out if your
BIG BROTHER
gets his hands
on your wand!

THE WAND WORKS WELL ON PETS OR STUFFED ANIMALS. ANY KIND WILL DO.

THE WAND SHOULD NEVER TOUCH YOUR PET'S EARS
OR THEY CAN GROW AS BIG AS AN ELEPHANT'S!

If there are no pets around, you might want to try the wand on a few bugs or frogs. It will work great!

You can also make good stuff to eat and drink. Try making the clouds into cotton candy or a glass of water into lemonade. This is a hard trick to do. It only works for people who have had a lot of practice, so keep trying!

The wand comes in handy when making the sky GREEN and the grass PURPLE and your car PEA GREEN with ORANGE and PINK polka dots!

Now, how do you take care of a magic wand? That's EASY!
If you were a magic wand, how would YOU like to be treated?
Would you like to be kicked around or stepped on? Would you
like to be left outside in the rain and mud? Of course not!

Always remember if you mistreat a magic wand, it could turn
into a troll or a leprechaun. Let's just say that the way we
fairies feel about trolls and leprechauns could fill a book!

I almost FORGOT to tell you about the most important part! A wand is given to you because you are very special and only the most special people of all can learn how to use it. A wand is only to be used by someone who has a good mind (to hold a large imagination), a great heart (to spread lots of joy and love) and a winsome spirit (to carry them their whole life through). That, my dear, describes you! Have FUN!

About the Author:

Carole LaPlante, nee Schmidt, is from Tinley Park, Illinois. She earned her Bachelors Degree in Elementary Education from Southwest Texas State University and her Masters Degree in Early Childhood from Bloomsburg University in Pennsylvania.

She has owned and operated her own childcare center, taught college courses in Ohio and Pennsylvania, and ESL in Cleveland, Turkey and Harrisburg, Pennsylvania, where she currently resides.

About the Illustrator:

Mary Ann Byrne-Walker is a native Pennsylvanian. She received her Bachelor's Degree from Penn State University and her Masters from University of St Francis. She is the illustrator of the children's book Night Noises.

Mary Ann currently resides with her husband and two children in Mechanicsburg Pennsylvania.